This book belongs to:

_____

DiRty BiRdy Feet

DiRty BiRdy Feet

by Rick Winter

illustrated by Mike Lester

rising moon

The illustrations were rendered in pencil and watercolor on vellum
The text type was set in Soup Bone
The display type was set in Ad Lib
Composed in the United States of America
Designed by Michael Russell
Edited by Aimee Jackson
Production supervised by Lisa Brownfield
Printed in Hong Kong by Midas Printing Limited

www.northlandpub.com

FIRST IMPRESSION
ISBN 0-87358-768-5
Library of Congress Catalog Card Number Pending

106/7.5M/8-00

To Mary Flowers,

my third grade teacher at Eastridge Elementary School.

You gave me my first journal and kindled a dream of writing.

With this book, I've realized the beginning of that dream.

—P. W.

To Hope,

Because she wants to.

—M. L.

One night we were eating dinner.

The whole family was at the table.

We were eating sloppy joes.

Mom had just washed the white carpet.

She told us to be careful.

A bird fell into the chimney.

It dropped into the ashes.

Little Sister and I watched.

Our cat dashed after the bird.

The bird flew all around.

Little Sister and I watched.

Our dog jogged after the cat.

The cat dashed.

The bird flew.

Little Sister

and I watched.

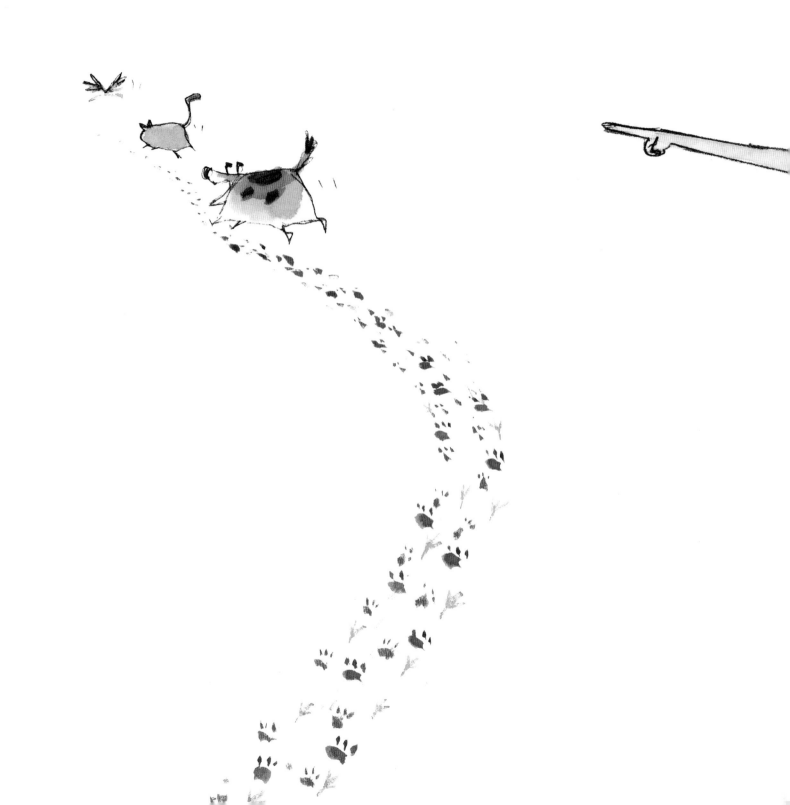

Mom yelled,

"Get those animals out of here, Son!"

Big Brother grabbed his sloppy joe

and dripped on the carpet.

The dog jogged.

The cat dashed.

The bird flew.

Little Sister and I watched.

Dad growled,

"Dumb dog!

Drat cat!

Dirty bird!"

Mom yelled,

"Get them, Son!"

Brother dripped.

The dog jogged.

The cat dashed.

The bird flew.

Little Sister

and I watched.

Mom raised her broom

and whooshed after them all.

Dad growled,

"Dumb dog!

Drat cat!

Dirty bird!"

Mom yelled,

"Get them, Son!"

Brother dripped.

The dog jogged.

The cat dashed.

The bird flew.

Little Sister

and I watched.

They all ran up the stairs.

Mom whooshed her broom.

Dad growled,

"Dumb dog!

Drat cat!

Dirty bird!"

Mom yelled,

"Get them, Son!"

Brother dripped.

The dog jogged.

The cat dashed.

The bird flew.

Little Sister and I watched.

The carpet wasn't white anymore.
Everywhere we could see
soot and sloppy joe
bird feet,
cat feet,
dog feet,
Brother feet,
Dad feet,
Mom feet.

They all raced
down the stairs.
Mom whooshed.

Dad growled,
"Dumb dog!
Drat cat!
Dirty bird!"
Mom yelled,
"Get them, Son!"
Brother dripped.
The dog jogged.
The cat dashed.
The bird flew.

Little Sister and I watched.

Mom yelled, "Open the door!"

I did.

Everyone charged outside.

The bird flew.

The cat dashed.

The dog jogged.

Brother dripped.

Dad growled.

Little Sister and I watched.

The bird screeched.

The cat yowled.

The dog howled.

Brother gobbled his sloppy joe.

And Dad growled.

Little Sister said,

"Do it again."

Rick Winter got the inspiration for *Dirty Birdy Feet* from his own rich childhood experiences, which included too many siblings, birds, dogs, cats, and various other animals (including an iguana, a spider monkey, and a parrot), and just the right number of parents (two). When Rick was about seven years old, his family sat down one night to what was supposed to be a quiet dinner, when a bird flopped down the chimney and into the ashes. Rick's mom—a very naive young mother then—had just cleaned the white carpet. The cat went after the bird and their normally calm and faithful dog, Lady, went after the cat.

Rick is the author of over forty computer books. *Dirty Birdy Feet* is his first book for children. He lives in Idaho Springs, Colorado, with his wife, Karen, and their two children, Danny and Jimmy.

Mike Lester was born in Atlanta, Georgia, and is a graduate of the University of Georgia. He has been a commercial illustrator for seventeen years and is the writer and creator of "Mike Du Jour," a daily animated cartoon appearing on dowjones.com. Mike has created corporate characters for several companies, including "Louie the Lightning Bug" for Georgia Power, "Christmas Reindeer" for Federal Express, and has illustrated ad campaigns for many corporations, including Blockbuster, Quaker Oats, Red Lobster, and Frito-Lay. He is also the creator of the sports mascot "Buz" the yellowjacket for Georgia Tech.

© 2000 Mark Law

Mike has illustrated over twenty books for children and is the writer and illustrator of *A is for Salad* (Penguin Putnam, March 2000). He lives in Rome, Georgia, with his wife, Cindy, and their children, Grady and Hope.